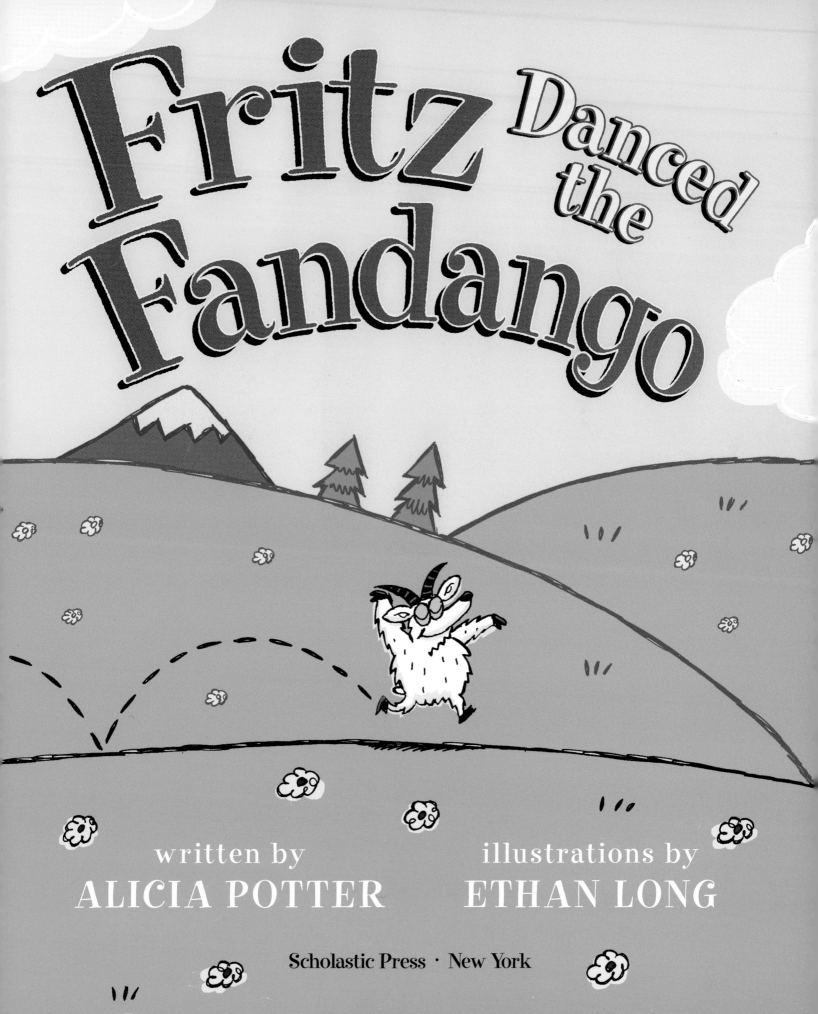

# Fritz Danced the Fandango

written by
**ALICIA POTTER**

illustrations by
**ETHAN LONG**

Scholastic Press · New York

Not many goats
danced the fandango . . .

but Fritz did.

He danced beneath the fir trees.

He danced among the heather.

He danced atop his favorite rock.

He loved the sound of his hooves.

## CLIP-CLIP-CLIPPETY-CLOP!

The other goats snickered.
They snorted.
They laughed their tails off.

Their snickers hurt Fritz's ears.

Their snorts made his hooves feel heavy.

Like they'd lost their clip.

And their clop.

"I don't belong with this herd," he said.

"I need to find some dancing goats."

Fritz imagined all the clipping.

He imagined all the clopping.

He imagined his pick of partners.

"Someday," thought Fritz, "I'll find my herd."
His heart fandangoed with hope.

So one morning, when the sun
was so bright, and the fields so buttercuppy,
Fritz couldn't stop his hooves.
He danced over the stile . . .

across the pasture . . .

and past the stream, until he couldn't hear
a single snicker or snort or laugh.

In a meadow,
he came upon a sheep named Liesl.
"Excuse me," said Fritz.
"But do you know any goats who
dance the fandango?"
"The fan-whato?" asked Liesl.

"The fandango," said Fritz.

He tossed off a few steps.

CLIP-CLIP-CLIPPETY-CLOP!

"Nope," said Liesl. "But I yodel.

YODEL-LAY-HEEEEEEEEEEEE-EWE!
YODELY-YODELY-HOO-HOO!"

"It's no fandango," she said, "but I like it.
The head ewe said it turned
her stomachs — all four of them — and so
I left the flock."

"Come with me," Fritz said.
"I'd like the company while I find a new herd."
"I'd be happy to!" said Liesl.

Fritz and Liesl shambled down ravines . . .
and gamboled up hills.

On the next alp,
they came upon a dog named
Gerhard, dozing in the shade.
"Pardon," said Fritz.
"But do you know any goats
who dance the fandango?"
"Fan-who?" asked Gerhard.

"The fandango." Fritz tossed off
a few steps.

**CLIP-CLIP-CLIPPETY-CLOP!**

"No," said Gerhard.
"But let me show *you* something."

He returned with a strange musical instrument.

"I play the glockenspiel," said Gerhard.

## PING-PING-A-LING-DING!

"It's no fandango," said Gerhard, "but it suits me.

Unfortunately, my shepherd said it distracts the flock."

"Come with us," Fritz said.

"We need some help finding my herd."

"At your service," said Gerhard.

Fritz, Liesl, and Gerhard
loped through pastures.

They climbed
and climbed.
And they practiced.

CLIP-CLIP-CLIPPETY-CLOP!
YODEL-LAY-HEEEEEEEEEEEE-EWE!
PING-PING-A-LING-DING!

They encountered many goats.
But not one danced the hokey-pokey,
never mind the fandango.

One day, Fritz wandered off,
alone and sad,
to the other side of a hill.

"There must be something we can do," said Gerhard.
"Yes," said Liesl. "But what?"

Liesl and Gerhard thought about
all the goats they'd ever met.
They thought about the most
musical beasts they knew.

"There's you," said Gerhard.
"And you," replied Liesl.
"But we've never
danced the fandango."

Fritz sighed. "Will I *ever* find my herd?
Am I destined to dance alone?"
His hooves felt heavy.
Like they'd lost their clip. And their clop.

But soon Fritz began to miss more
than a dancing partner. He missed Liesl and Gerhard.

Just then, a sound wafted to Fritz's ears.

It was the sound of hooves. Dancing hooves.

"Could it be?" whispered Fritz.

Fritz galloped up . . . up . . . up the hill.

At the top he found . . .

. . . Liesl and Gerhard dancing the fandango!

"How did you learn to dance like that?" asked Fritz.

"We watched you so often . . ." panted Gerhard.

". . . We taught ourselves," finished Liesl.

Fritz, Liesl, and Gerhard fandangoed

like there was no tomorrow.

They **CLIP-CLIP-CLIPPETY-CLOPPED!**

They **YODEL-LAY-HEEEEEEEEEEE-EWED!**

They even took turns **PING-PING-A-LINGING**
on Gerhard's glockenspiel.

The trio made quite a ruckus on the buttercuppy hills.

Fritz sighed.

"Finally, I've found my herd!" he said.

His heart fandangoed with joy.

Library of Congress Cataloging-in-Publication Data Available

ISBN-13: 978-0-545-07554-1
ISBN-10: 0-545-07554-8

10 9 8 7 6 5 4 3 2 1      09 10 11 12 13

Printed in Singapore   46
First edition, May 2009

Book design by Christopher Stengel

To my mother and father,
Cecilie and Arthur Potter,
with a mountain of love
–A.P.

To all my friends at
Princeton Elementary School
–E.L.